Tractor Rescue

Illustrated by Steve Smallman

First published by Parragon in 2012
Parragon
Queen Street House
4 Queen Street
Bath BA1 1HE, UK
www.parragon.com

Written by; Gaby Goldsack
Illustrated by; Steve Smallman

ISBN 978-1-4454-9526-2

Printed in China

Tractor
Rescue

PaRragon

Bath • New York • Singapore • Hong Kong • Cologne • Delhi
Melbourne • Amsterdam • Johannesburg • Shenzhen

One morning, Farmer Fred was very excited. His new turbo-charged quad bike had just arrived.

He raced it up the farm track and skidded to a halt in front of his wife Jenny.

"This is going to get me around the farm far faster than the tractor," he said proudly. "I might even get rid of the tractor!"

"Woof, woof," barked Patch the sheep dog.
He wasn't at all sure he liked this new machine.

Later that morning, Farmer Fred used the quad bike to check on the sheep. Then he used it to carry a bale of hay out to the meadow. And at milking time, he used it to bring in the cows.

Farmer Fred didn't use the tractor at all that day. And he didn't use it the day after that, or the day after that. The poor tractor just sat in the barn gathering dust. Then Farmer Fred began using it as a store cupboard. First he hung a coil of rope around its exhaust. Then he stuffed the cab full of old machine parts.

"Neigh," sighed Harry the horse. He thought the tractor looked very sad.

Later that week Farmer Fred was waiting for his Aunt Mabel to arrive, when Jenny rushed out of the farmhouse. "Your Aunt Mabel has just phoned," she told him. "Her car is stuck in a pothole on the farm track. Can you go and pull her out?"

"Leaping lettuces," cried Farmer Fred, jumping onto his quad bike. "Poor old Aunt Mabel. Come on, Patch. Let's go and rescue her."

"Woof, woof," barked Patch, racing over to the tractor.

"Good thinking," cried Farmer Fred. "Fetch me that rope. It's just what we need to pull Aunt Mabel's car to safety."

Farmer Fred and Patch were soon at Aunt Mabel's side. Her little car was well and truly stuck in a muddy pothole.

"Get me out of here," wailed Aunt Mabel.

"Don't worry," called Farmer Fred, as he tied one end of the rope to the car's bumper.

"My new quad bike will have you out of there in a jiffy."

Farmer Fred tied the other end of the rope to his quad bike and leapt on. He revved the engine and jumped up and down but nothing happened. Aunt Mabel's car would not budge. It was well and truly stuck in the mud.

Farmer Fred turned off the engine and scratched his head. If his turbo-charged quad bike couldn't pull Aunt Mabel's car to safety, what could? As he wondered what to do, Harry Horse came to see what was happening.

"Aha," cried Farmer Fred. "Patch, fetch Harry's harness. I'll tie this rope to Harry and he can pull the car out."

But although Harry pulled and pulled with all his strength, the car would not budge. It was well and truly stuck in the mud.

Next Farmer Fred got all the animals to push the car as hard as they could. "Heave-ho," cried Farmer Fred. The engine roared. The wheels whizzed round. Everyone got splattered with mud. But the car would not budge. It was well and truly stuck in the mud.

And it wouldn't move when Farmer Fred tried to dig it out. Or when he tried to lever it out. Or even when he tried to wash it out with his pressure washer. In fact, it just got more and more stuck.

Farmer Fred carried Aunt Mabel to safety. And then drove her up to the farmhouse on his quad bike.
"But what about my little car?" asked Aunt Mabel.

Patch ran up to the tractor and began to bark. Suddenly Farmer Fred had an idea.

"Never fear, I've an idea," cried Farmer Fred cheerfully. And he grabbed a box of machine parts from the tractor.

Farmer Fred dashed off to his workshop and disappeared inside. As he banged and crashed around, the animals gathered round outside.

"What do you think he is doing?" mooed Connie Cow.

"Quack, quack, quack," wailed Dotty Duck, running round and round in circles.

"Woof, woof," barked Patch. "I just wish he'd listen to me. I know what could pull the car to safety – the tr...

But the other animals were far too busy talking to listen.

Before long, Farmer Fred came out of the workshop holding some cogs and a plank of wood tied onto some rope.

"This," Farmer Fred said grandly, "is my PULLEY-OUTER."

Farmer Fred attached the PULLEY-OUTER to his quad bike and started the engine. The quad bike's engine roared. The PULLEY-OUTER whirred and turned. The car creaked and groaned.

Everyone held their breath as the car started to move. But then there was a loud CREAK, followed by a SNAP as the rope broke. Cogs flew this way and that. The animals dashed for cover. And Farmer Fred was almost knocked off the quad bike by a flying plank of wood.

Luckily, no-one was hurt. But there was a loud SLURP as the car sank deeper into the mud.

"Catapulting cabbages," cried Farmer Fred. "I don't think we're ever going to get Aunt Mabel's car out."

"Woof, woof," barked Patch, tugging at Farmer Fred's sleeve.

"What is it, boy?" asked Farmer Fred. "Do you want me to follow you?"

Fred followed Patch back to the farmyard and into the barn.

"Woof, woof," barked Patch. He jumped up and down in front of the tractor.

"Of course," cried Farmer Fred. "The tractor will easily pull Aunt Mabel's car to safety."

Everyone cheered as the tractor pulled Aunt Mabel's car out of the muddy pothole.

"There's nothing quite like a tractor," said Farmer Fred. "I don't think I'll get rid of it, after all."
"Perhaps you can use it to mend some of the potholes on your farm track," said Aunt Mabel.

"Err, maybe," said Farmer Fred.
Jenny looked at Patch and laughed.

THE END